To Nicholas

From the "Nesseltops"

Christmas 2000

JEAN DE BRUNHOFF
BONJOUR, BABAR!

The Six Unabridged Classics by the Creator of Babar

With an Introduction by Kevin Henkes

Random House 🏠 New York

www.randomhouse.com/kids

Library of Congress Cataloging-in-Publication Data
Brunhoff, Jean de, 1899–1937.
Bonjour, Babar!: the six unabridged classics by the creator of Babar / by Jean de Brunhoff ;
with an introduction by Kevin Henkes.
p. cm.
SUMMARY: Six tales chronicling the life and adventures of Babar the elephant including
"The story of Babar," "The travels of Babar," "Babar the king," "Babar and Zephir,"
"Babar and his children," and "Babar and Father Christmas."
ISBN 0-375-81060-9   [1. Elephants—Fiction.] I. Henkes, Kevin.
II. Title.   PZ7.B828428 Bo 2000   [E]—dc21   00-038709

Printed in the United States of America   September 2000   10 9 8 7 6 5 4 3 2 1

TABLE OF CONTENTS

Introduction by KEVIN HENKES 8

INTRODUCTION

by KEVIN HENKES

Jean de Brunhoff did many cover sketches for his first book before settling on the one pictured above, which also incorporates his hand-lettering.

I see Babar every day. He is lying in the Old Lady's bathtub, washing himself with a yellow sponge. The tub is overflowing with elephant and water. The illustration is from *The Story of Babar* and is printed on a postcard that is taped to the wall in my family's bathroom. I come out of the shower—and there is Babar. I look in the mirror as I shave—there he is again. I fetch a glass of water for one of my children late at night—Babar is watching. The postcard has been hanging in its spot for nearly ten years. It is curling at the edges, marked by splashes, a bit discolored, and freckled with mold. But to take Babar down from the wall would be like removing a cherished family photograph. I remember the image from my childhood.

I had little exposure to art as a child, except, of course, art found in books. I returned to the illustrations I loved time and time again. I returned to Crockett Johnson, Garth Williams, and Maurice Sendak. I returned to Jean de Brunhoff. I returned to Babar.

The Babar books I remember were library books. And many of the things I sought as a young artist and writer could be found in those books.

I remember thick, creamy paper; rich, saturated color; and, in some of the editions I had access to, hand-lettering that intrigued me no end.

I usually chose my library books based on the illustrations in them, but the Babar books had much to offer, art aside. Where else could one find a balloon accident, a deadly poison mushroom, a runaway carriage, an extraordinary flying machine, a snake attack, fire, war, death, birth? These books are full of adventure and fantasy, but they also deal with the stuff of real life. And I'm convinced children long to see both the dark and the light sides of human experience reflected in their books just as much as adults do, perhaps more.

Nearly twenty years have passed since my first book was published. And it was forty-eight years before that that *The Story of Babar* appeared. Commercial printing techniques have changed dramatically since Babar's debut, some would say improved dramatically. And yet there are few who can rival Mr. de Brunhoff's sure line, elegant use of color, and grasp of design, which is to envy.

Two of his double spreads in particular—the circus from *The Travels of Babar* and the theater in the Amusement Park from *Babar the King*—are spectacular. Simple, direct, complete.

The nurse in *Babar and His Children* makes a cradle out of a wash basket, a towel, and an umbrella. And Cornelius makes a swing for Alexander by hanging rope between his tusks. Details like these—witty, original, logical—add resonance.

And has black-and-white ever looked richer than in the illustration showing the King and Queen from behind on their wedding night? The two crowns glow like jagged moons in a sky crowded with stars. Celeste's veil and gown glow as well, as if she is illuminated from within. Their outlines reach high into the sky and echo the shape of the distant hills. Babar and Celeste are part of both the landscape and the heavens. Grounded and elevated. Solid and luminous. Perfection.

Mr. de Brunhoff celebrated the family—one of the wells I mine on a regular basis. *Babar and His Children* is one of my favorite books about family life. The joy, the drama, the pandemonium—they are all there, along with artistry, humor, and substance. The eight-panel sequence in which Flora chokes on her rattle and is finally saved by Zephir is unflinching. As often happens when reading these books, we forget we're thinking about animals and we see loved ones, we see ourselves.

I have a clear childhood memory of running my finger along the curving line of elephants on the mirror-image

(from right to left) Cécile de Brunhoff and her sons, Mathieu and Laurent, in 1931, shortly after the first Babar story was created.

Jean de Brunhoff, photographed in September 1930 at the very time he was creating Babar.

These designs were created by Jean de Brunhoff to decorate the children's dining room in the famous French transatlantic liner the *Normandie*. They were cut out of wood and mounted on the green walls.

endsheets that appear in all the Babar books. Thirty-some years later I've seen my own children do the same thing, independent of each other, and unprompted by me. I'm sure other children had done this before I had, and I'm sure others will do it long after my children have grown up and moved on. The magic has traveled from generation to generation, and will continue to do so.

At the end of *Babar and His Children*, after a particularly exhausting day with Pom, Flora, and Alexander, Babar says, "Truly it is not easy to bring up a family." The same could be said for creating a good book.

Despite the exhausting day, Babar concludes that babies are nice. "I wouldn't know how to get along without them any more," he says.

And how would we get along without these books?

Thank goodness we don't have to worry about that.

Kevin Henkes
Madison, Wisconsin
September 2000

This drawing was one of many early sketches Jean de Brunhoff made for *The Story of Babar*. It illustrates the opening scene, in which Babar's mother is killed by a hunter. The action, shown here all on one page, was ultimately broken into two separate pages.

JEAN DE BRUNHOFF

THE STORY
OF
BABAR
the little elephant

Translated from the French by Merle S. Haas

Random House New York

In the great forest a little elephant is born. His name is Babar. His mother loves him very much. She rocks him to sleep with her trunk while singing softly to him.

Babar has grown bigger. He now plays with the other little elephants. He

is a very good little elephant. See him digging in the sand with his shell.

Babar is riding happily on his mother's back when
a wicked hunter, hidden behind some bushes,
shoots at them.

The hunter has killed Babar's mother! The
monkey hides, the birds fly away, Babar cries.
The hunter runs up to catch poor Babar.

Babar runs away because he is afraid of the hunter. After several days, very tired indeed, he comes to a town . . .

He hardly knows what to make of it because this is the first time that he has seen so many houses.

So many things are new to him! The broad
streets! The automobiles and buses! However, he
is especially interested in two gentlemen he
notices on the street.

He says to himself: "Really, they are very well
dressed. I would like to have some fine clothes,
too! I wonder how I can get them?"

Luckily, a very rich Old Lady who has always been fond of little elephants understands right away that he is longing for a fine suit. As she likes to make people happy, she gives him her purse. Babar says to her politely: "Thank you, Madam."

Without wasting any time, Babar goes into a big store. He enters the elevator. It is such fun to ride up and down in this funny box, that he rides all the way up ten times and all the way down ten times. He did not want to stop but the elevator boy finally said to him: "This is not a toy, Mr. Elephant. You must get out and do your shopping. Look, here is the floorwalker."

23

Babar then

a shirt
with a collar
and tie,

a suit of a
becoming shade
of green,

buys himself:

then a
handsome
derby hat,

and also
shoes with
spats.

25

Well satisfied with his purchases
and feeling very elegant indeed,
Babar now goes to the photog-
rapher to have his picture taken.

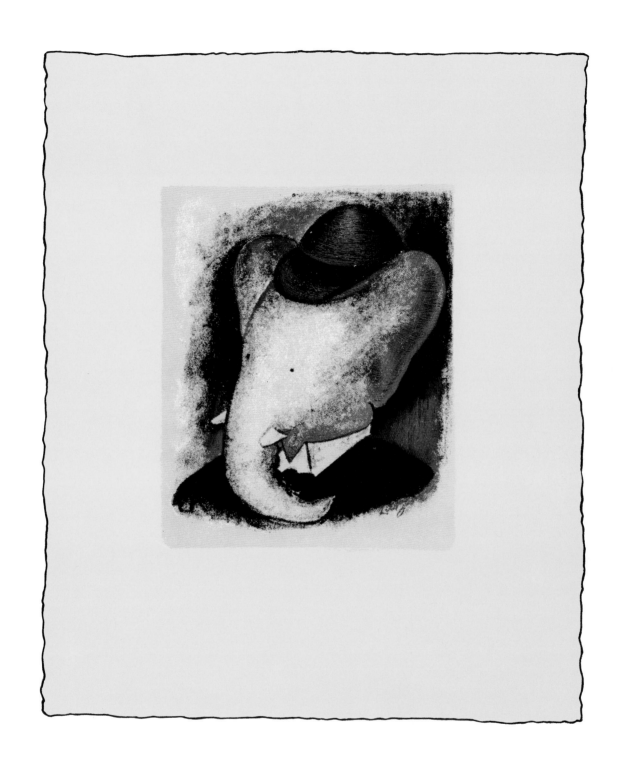

And here is his photograph.

Babar dines with his friend the Old Lady. She thinks he looks very smart in his new clothes. After dinner, because he is tired, he goes to bed and falls asleep very quickly.

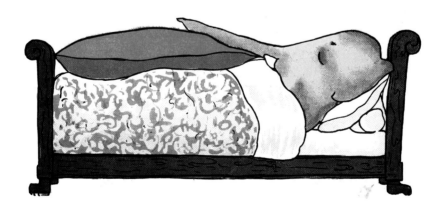

Babar now lives at the Old Lady's house.
In the mornings, he does setting-up exercises with her, and then he takes his bath.

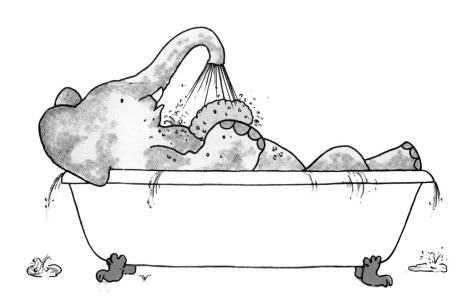

He goes out for an automobile ride every day. The Old Lady has given him the car. She gives him whatever he wants.

A learned professor gives him lessons. Babar pays attention and does well in his work. He is a good pupil and makes rapid progress.

In the evening, after dinner, he tells the Old Lady's friends all about his life in the great forest.

However, Babar is not quite happy, for he misses playing in the great forest with his little cousins and his friends, the monkeys. He often stands at the window, thinking sadly of his childhood, and cries when he remembers his mother.

Two years have passed. One day during his walk
he sees two little elephants coming toward him.
They have no clothes on. "Why," he says in
astonishment to the Old Lady, "it's Arthur and
Celeste, my little cousins!"

Babar kisses them affectionately and hurries
off with them to buy them some fine clothes.

He takes them to a pastry shop to eat some good cakes.

Meanwhile, in the forest, the elephants are calling and hunting high and low for Arthur and Celeste, and their mothers are worried.

Fortunately, in flying over the town, an old marabou bird has seen them and comes back quickly to tell the news.

The mothers of Arthur and Celeste have come
to the town to fetch them. They are very happy
to have them back, but they scold them just the
same because they ran away.

Babar makes up his mind to go back with Arthur
and Celeste and their mothers to see the great
forest again. The Old Lady helps him to pack
his trunk.

They are all ready to start. Babar kisses the Old Lady good-bye. He would be quite happy to go if it were not for leaving her. He promises to come back some day. He will never forget her.

They have gone. . . . There is no room in the car for the mothers, so they run behind, and lift up their trunks to avoid breathing the dust. The Old Lady is left alone. Sadly she wonders: "When shall I see my little Babar again?"

Alas, that very day, the King of the elephants
had eaten a bad mushroom.

It poisoned him and he became ill, so ill that he died. This was a great calamity.

After the funeral the three oldest elephants were holding a meeting to choose a new King.

Just then they hear a noise. They turn around. Guess what they see! Babar arriving in his car and all the elephants running and shouting: "Here they are! Here they are! Hello, Babar! Hello, Arthur! Hello, Celeste! What beautiful clothes! What a beautiful car!"

Then Cornelius, the oldest of all the elephants, spoke in his quavering voice: "My good friends, we are seeking a King. Why not choose Babar? He has just returned from the big city, he has learned so much living among men, let us crown him King." All the other elephants thought that Cornelius had spoken wisely and eagerly they await Babar's reply.

"I want to thank you one and all," said Babar, "but before accepting your proposal, I must explain to you that, while we were traveling in the car, Celeste and I became engaged. If I become your King, she will be your Queen."

"Long live Queen Celeste!

Long live King Babar!"

cry all the elephants without a moment's hesitation. And thus it was that Babar became King.

"You have good ideas," said Babar to Cornelius.
"I will therefore make you a general, and when
I get my crown, I will give you my hat. In a week
I shall marry Celeste. We will then have a
splendid party in honor of our marriage and our
coronation." Then, turning to the birds, Babar
asks them to go and invite all the animals to the
festivities, and he tells the dromedary to go to the

town and buy some beautiful wedding clothes.

The wedding guests begin to arrive. The dromedary returns with the bridal costumes just in the
nick of time for the ceremony.

After the wedding and the coronation

everybody dances merrily.

The festivities are over, night has fallen, the stars
have risen in the sky. King Babar and Queen Celeste
are indeed very happy.

Now the world is asleep. The guests have gone home, happy, though tired from too much dancing. They will long remember this great celebration.

And now King Babar and Queen Celeste, both eager for further adventures, set out on their honeymoon in a gorgeous yellow balloon.

JEAN DE BRUNHOFF

THE TRAVELS
of
BABAR

Translated from the French by Merle S. Haas
Random House New York

Babar, the young King of the elephants, and his wife, Queen Celeste, have just left for their wedding trip in a balloon.

"Good-by! See you soon!" cry the elephants as they watch the balloon rise and drift away.

Arthur, Babar's little cousin, still waves his beret. Old Cornelius, who is chief over all the elephants when the King is away, anxiously sighs: "I do hope they won't have any accidents!"

The country of the elephants is now far away.
The balloon glides noiselessly in the sky. Babar
and Celeste admire the landscape below. What
a beautiful journey! The air is balmy, the wind
is gentle. There is the ocean, the big blue ocean.

Blown out over the sea by the wind, the balloon is suddenly caught by a violent storm. Babar and Celeste tremble with fear and cling with all their might to the basket of the balloon.

By extraordinary good fortune, just as the balloon is about to fall into the sea, a final puff of wind blows it on an island where it flattens out and collapses.

"You aren't hurt, Celeste, are you?" Babar inquires anxiously. "No! Well then look, we are saved!"

Leaving the wrecked balloon on the beach, Babar and Celeste pick up their belongings and go off to seek shelter.

Having found a quiet spot, they take off their clothes. Celeste hangs them up to dry, while Babar lights a good fire and prepares breakfast.

Babar and Celeste settle themselves comfortably. They have set up their tent and, sitting on some large stones, they eat with relish an excellent rice broth well-sweetened and cooked to perfection. "We are not so badly off on this island," says Babar.

After breakfast, while Babar explores the surrounding country, Celeste, left alone, falls sound asleep.

Just then, the inhabitants of the island, fierce and savage cannibals, suddenly discover her.

"What kind of strange beast is this?" they say to one another. "We have never seen anything like it. Its meat must be very tender. Let's creep up quietly and catch it while it sleeps."

The cannibals have succeeded in tying up Celeste with the clothesline on which the clothes were drying. Some dance with joy, while others have great fun trying on the stolen garments. Celeste sighs sadly, she thinks soon she will be eaten. She does not yet see Babar, who returns just in time to save her!

In the twinkling of an eye, Babar has unbound
Celeste. They both hurl themselves on the cannibals. Some are wounded, others take flight; all
are terrified.

Only a few courageous ones still resist. But they are thinking: "These big animals are certainly terribly strong and their hides are mighty tough!"

After having chased off the savages, Babar and Celeste rest themselves on the seashore. Suddenly, right in front of them a whale comes to the surface and spouts. Babar gets up immediately and says:

"Good morning, Mrs. Whale, I am Babar, King of the elephants, and here is my wife Celeste. We have had a balloon accident and have fallen here on this island. Could you help us to get away?"

"I am delighted to make your acquaintance,"
answers the whale, "and I will be very happy if
I can be of service to you. I am just leaving to
visit my family in the Arctic Ocean. I will drop
you wherever you like. Quick, get on my back
and hold tight so you don't slip off. Are you
ready? Get set. Let's go!"

A few days later, a little weary, they are resting on a reef. Just then a school of little fish
swims by.

"I am going to eat up some of these," says the
whale. "I'll be back in a minute." And she dives
down after them.

The whale has not come back! While eating the little fish, she completely forgot her new friends. She is a giddy, thoughtless creature.

"We were better off on the cannibal island. What will become of us now?" weeps poor Celeste. Babar does his best to comfort her.

After hours and hours spent on their little reef, without even a drop of fresh water, they finally spy a ship passing quite near them. She is a big steamer with three funnels. Babar and Celeste call out and yell as loudly as they can, but no one hears them. They try signaling with their trunks and with their arms. Oh, will they attract someone's attention?

They have been seen! A lifeboat rescues them
while the excited passengers all watch.

A week later, the huge ship

steams slowly into a big harbor.

All the passengers go down the gangplank. Babar and Celeste would like to follow too but they are not allowed to. They have lost their crowns during the storm, so no one will believe that they are actually King and Queen of the elephants, and the Captain of the ship orders them locked up in the ship's stables.

"They give us straw to sleep on!" cries Babar angrily. "We are fed hay, as though we were donkeys! The door is locked! I've had enough of this, I'm going to smash everything."

"Be quiet, I beg you," says Celeste, "I hear someone. It is the Captain coming into the stable. Let's be good so he'll let us out."

"Here are my elephants," says the Captain to the famous animal trainer, Fernando, who is with him. "I cannot keep them on my ship; I give them to you for your circus."

Fernando thanks the Captain and leads away
his two new pupils.

"Be patient, Babar," whispers Celeste, "we will
not remain long with the circus. We will get back
to our native land again somehow and see Cornelius and little Arthur."

Now just at this time, back in the elephants' country, little Arthur has had a mischievous idea. While Rataxes the rhinoceros was having a quiet siesta, Arthur tied a big firecracker to his tail without waking him. The firecracker explodes with a terrific bang and Rataxes leaps up into the air. Arthur, the scamp, laughs until he nearly chokes. It is really a very mean trick.

Rataxes is furious. Cornelius, very worried, goes
to find him and says:

"My dear fellow, I am so sorry. Arthur will be
severely punished. He begs for your forgiveness."

"Get away, old Cornelius," grumbles Rataxes.
"Don't speak to me of that scoundrel, Arthur. You
elephants may think you have made fun of me but
just wait – you'll soon see!"

"What will he do?" wonders Cornelius. "I feel
very uneasy; he is revengeful and mean. Ah! If only
Babar were here!"

But Babar is now far away playing the trumpet

while Celeste dances in Fernando's circus.

One day the circus comes to the town where Babar, when he was young, had met his friend the Old Lady. So, at night, while Fernando is in bed, Babar and Celeste escape and go to find her, for he has never forgotten her.

Babar finds the house easily and rings the bell.
The Old Lady awakes, puts on her wrapper, steps
out on her balcony and calls:

"Who's there?"

"Babar and Celeste," they answer her.

The Old Lady is overjoyed. She has really be-
lieved she would never see them again. Babar and
Celeste are happy, too, for they will never have
to go back to the circus. Soon they will be able
to rejoin Arthur and Cornelius. The Old Lady
has promised to help them.

The Old Lady lends Celeste a nightgown and provides Babar with a pair of pajamas. They have just awakened after a sound sleep. Now they are having breakfast in bed for they are still quite tired after all their adventures.

At the circus, their escape has just been discovered.

"Stop! Thief! My elephants have been stolen!" cries the excited Fernando.

"Little ones, oh little ones, where are you hiding?" the clowns repeat, and look everywhere for them.

Babar and Celeste will not be caught again. Here they are on their way to the station with the Old Lady. They need a few days' rest before returning to their own land. So the three of them are going to the mountains to enjoy the fresh air and try a little skiing.

Now Babar and Celeste have packed away their
skis and said good-by to the mountains. They are
leaving by plane to return home. The Old Lady
accompanies them. Babar has invited her, as he
is anxious to show her his beautiful country and
the great forest where one always hears the birds
singing.

They have landed. The airplane has gone back.
Babar and Celeste are speechless with surprise.
Where are Cornelius, Arthur, and the other elephants? A few broken trees! Is that all that is left
of the great forest? There are no more flowers,
no more birds. Babar and Celeste are very sad
and weep as they see their ruined country. The
Old Lady understands their grief.

"What is going on here?" inquiries Babar, who has found the other elephants at last.

"Alas!" replies Cornelius. "The rhinoceroses have declared war on us. They came led by Rataxes who wanted to catch Arthur and make mincemeat of him! We tried bravely to protect the little fellow, but the rhinoceroses were too strong for us. We do not know how to drive them off."

"This is indeed bad news," says Babar, "but let's not give up."

But real war is not a joke, and many of the elephants have been wounded. Celeste and the Old Lady take care of them with great devotion. The Old Lady is especially good at this, as she used to be a trained nurse. Babar and some of the soldiers who have recovered have gone back to the front with Cornelius to join the elephant army. The rhinoceroses are preparing to attack. A big battle will soon begin!

Here is the camp of the rhinoceroses. The soldiers are awaiting orders, and think: "We will once again defeat the elephants, then the war will be over and we can all go home." Spiteful old Rataxes maliciously says to his friend General Pamir: "Hah! Hah! Hah! Pretty soon we will tweak the ears of this young King Babar and punish that rascal Arthur."

Here is the camp of the elephants. They have all found new courage. And now Babar has a bright idea:

He disguises his biggest soldiers, painting their tails bright red, and near their tails on either side he paints large, frightening eyes. Arthur sets to work making wigs. He works as hard as he can so he'll be forgiven for causing all this trouble.

The day of the battle, at just the right moment the disguised elephants come out of hiding.
And Babar's bright idea succeeds!

The rhinoceroses think they are monsters and, terrified, they retreat in great disorder. King Babar is a mighty fine general.

The rhinoceroses have fled and are still running. Pamir and Rataxes are prisoners, and hang their heads in shame. What a glorious day for the elephants! In chorus they all cry:

"Bravo, Babar—Bravo! Victory! Victory! The war is over! How perfectly splendid!"

The next day before all the elephants, Babar
and Celeste, having put on their royal garments
and their new crowns, reward the Old Lady who
has been so good to them and has cared so well
for the wounded. They give her eleven singing
canaries and a cunning little monkey.

After the ceremony, Babar, Celeste and the
Old Lady sit and chat under the palm trees.
"And what are we going to do next?" asks the
Old Lady.

"I am going to try to rule my kingdom wisely," answers Babar, "and if you will remain with
us, you can help me make my subjects happy."

JEAN DE BRUNHOFF

BABAR
THE KING

Translated from the French by Merle S. Haas
Random House New York

Off in the country of the elephants King Babar and Queen
Celeste are rejoicing: they have signed a treaty of peace with
the rhinoceros, and their friend, the Old Lady, has consented
to remain with them. She often tells the elephants' children
stories; her little monkey, Zephir, perched up in a tree, also
listens.

Leaving the Old Lady with Queen Celeste, Babar has gone for a walk along the banks of a large lake with Cornelius, the oldest and wisest of all the elephants, and he says to him, "This countryside is so beautiful that I would like to see it every day

as I wake up. We must build our city here. Our houses shall be on the shores of the lake, and shall be surrounded with flowers and birds." Zephir, who has followed them, would like to catch a butterfly he sees . . . .

While chasing the butterfly, Zephir meets his friend
Arthur, the young cousin of the King and Queen, who
was amusing himself hunting for snails. All of a sudden
they see one, two, three, four dromedaries . . . five, six,
seven dromedaries . . . eight, nine, ten . . . . There are more
than they can count. And the chief of the cavalcade calls to
them: "Can you please tell us where we can find King
Babar?"

Escorted by Arthur and Zephir, the dromedaries have found Babar. They are bringing him all his heavy baggage and all the things which he had bought out in the big world, during his honeymoon. Babar thanks them: "You must be tired, gentlemen. Won't you rest under the shade of the palm trees?" Then, turning to the Old Lady and to Cornelius, he says: "Now we will be able to build our city."

Having called an assembly of all the elephants, Babar climbs up on a packing case and, in a loud voice, proclaims the following words: "My friends, I have in these trunks, these bales, and these sacks, gifts for each of you. There are dresses, suits, hats and materials, paint boxes, drums, fishing tackle and rods, ostrich feathers, tennis rackets and many other things. I will divide all this among you as soon as we have finished building our city. This city—the city of the elephants — I would like to suggest that we name Celesteville, in honor of your Queen."

All the elephants raised their trunks and cried: "What a good idea! What an excellent idea!"

The elephants set to work quickly. Arthur and Zephir
hand out the tools. Babar tells each one what he should do.
He marks with sign-boards where the streets and houses
should go. He orders some to cut down trees, some to move
stones; others saw wood or dig holes. With what joy they
all strive to do their best! The Old Lady is playing the
phonograph for them and from time to time Babar plays
on his trumpet; he is fond of music. All the elephants are
as happy as he is. They drive nails, draw logs, pull and
push, dig, fetch and carry, opening their big ears wide as
they work.

Over in the big lake the fish are complaining among themselves: "We can't even sleep peacefully any longer," they say. "These elephants make the most dreadful noise! What are they building? When we jump out of the water we really haven't time to see clearly. We'll have to ask the frogs what it is all about."

The birds also gathered together to discuss what the elephants were up to. The pelicans and the flamingos, the ducks and the ibis and even the smaller birds all twittered, chirruped and quacked, and the parrots enthusiastically kept repeating: "Come and see Celesteville, the most beautiful of all cities! Come and see Celesteville, the most beautiful of all cities!"

Here is Celesteville! The elephants have just finished building it
and are resting or bathing. Babar goes for a sail with Arthur
and Zephir. He is well satisfied, and admires his new capital.
Each elephant has his own house. The Old Lady's is at the

upper left, the one for the King and Queen is at the upper right. The big lake is visible from all their windows. The Bureau of Industry is next door to the Amusement Hall which will be very practical and convenient.

Today Babar keeps his promise. He gives a gift to each elephant and also serviceable clothes suitable for work-days and beautiful rich clothes for holidays. After thanking their King most heartily, the elephants all go home dancing with glee.

Babar has decided that next Sunday all the elephants will dress up in their best clothes and assemble in the gardens of the Amusement Park. The gardeners have much to do. They rake the paths, water the flower beds and set out the last flower pots.

The elephant children are planning a surprise for Babar and Celeste. They have asked Cornelius to teach them the song of the elephants. Arthur had the idea. They are very attentive, keep time, and will know it perfectly by Sunday.

SONG OF THE ELEPHANTS

MELODY

Pa- ta- li di- ra- pa- ta crom- da crom- da ri- pa- lo

REFRAIN :

Pa- ta Pa- ta ko ko ko

WORDS

1st VERSE

PATALI DIRAPATA
CROMDA CROMDA RIPALO
PATA PATA
KO KO KO

2nd VERSE

BOKORO DIPOULITO
RONDI RONDI PEPINO
PATA PATA
KO KO KO

3rd VERSE

EMANA KARASSOLI
LOUCRA LOUCRA PONPONTO
PATA PATA
KO KO KO

NOTE: This song is the old chant of the Mammoths.
Cornelius himself doesn't know what the words mean —

The cooks are hurriedly preparing cakes and dainties of all kinds. Queen Celeste comes to help them. Zephir comes too, with Arthur. He tastes the vanilla cream to see if it is just right; first he puts in his finger, then his hand, and then his arm. Arthur is dying of envy and would like to stick his trunk in it.

In order to have one last taste Zephir bends his head, sticks out his tongue and *plouf!*—in he falls head first. At this sound the chief cook looks around and, greatly annoyed, fishes him out by the tail. The soup chef bursts out laughing. Arthur hides. Poor little Zephir is a sight, all yellow and sticky. Celeste scolds him and goes off to clean him up.

Sunday comes at last. In the gardens of the Amusement Park the elephants saunter about dressed magnificently. The children have sung their song, Babar has kissed each one. The cakes

were delicious! What a wonderful day! Unfortunately, it is over all too soon. The Old Lady is already organizing the last round of hide-and-seek.

The next day after their morning dip in the lake, the children go to school. And they are glad to find their dear teacher, the Old Lady, waiting for them. Lessons are never tiresome when she teaches.

After having settled the little ones at their tasks, she turns

her attention to the older ones, and asks them: "Two times two?" — "Three," answers Arthur. "No, no, four," said his neighbor Ottilie. "For, that's what we study for," sang Zephir. "Four," repeated Arthur. "I'll not forget that again, teacher."

All the elephants who are too old to attend classes, have chosen a trade. For example: Tapitor is a cobbler, Pilophage an officer, Capoulosse is a doctor, Barbacol a tailor, Podular a sculptor and Hatchibombotar is a street cleaner. Doulamor is a musician, Olur is a mechanic, Poutifour a farmer, Fandago is a learned man. Justinien is a painter and Coco a clown. If Capoulosse has holes in his shoes, he brings them to Tapitor, and, if Tapitor is sick, Capoulosse takes care of him. If Barbacol wants a statue for his mantelpiece, he asks Podular to carve one for him, and when Podular's coat is worn out Barbacol makes a new one to order for him. Justinien paints a portrait of Pilophage, who will protect him against his enemies. Hatchibombotar cleans the streets, Olur repairs the automobiles, and, when they are all tired, Doulamor plays his cello to entertain them. After having settled grave problems, Fandago relaxes and eats some of Poutifour's fruits. As for Coco, he keeps them all laughing and gay.

At Celesteville, all the elephants work in the morning, and in the afternoon they can do as they please. They play, go for walks, read and dream . . . . Babar and Celeste like to play tennis with Mr. and Mrs. Pilophage.

Cornelius, Fandago, Podular and Capoulosse prefer to play bowls. The children play with Coco, the clown. Arthur and Zephir have put on masks. There is a shallow pool in which to sail their boats and there are many other games besides.

But what the elephants like best of all

is the theater in the Amusement Park.

Every day, early in the morning, Hatchibombotar sprinkles the streets with his motor sprinkler. When Arthur and Zephir meet him, they quickly take off their shoes, and run after the car, barefoot. "Oh, what a fine shower!" they say laughingly. Unfortunately, Babar caught them at it one day. "No dessert for either of you, you rascals!" he cried.

Arthur and Zephir are mischievous, as are all little boys, but they are not lazy. Babar and Celeste visit the Old Lady, and are amazed to hear them play the violin and cello. "It is wonderful!" says Celeste, and Babar adds: "My dear children, I am indeed pleased with you. Go to the pastry shop and select whatever cakes you like."

Arthur and Zephir are very happy to have had all the
cakes they wanted, but they are even more delighted when
at the distribution of prizes, they hear Cornelius read out:
"First prize for music: a tie between Arthur and Zephir."
Very proudly, with wreaths on their heads, they went back
to their seats. After having rewarded the good scholars,
Cornelius made a noble speech.

"... And now I wish you all a pleasant holiday!" he ended up. Everyone clapped hard and applauded loudly. Then, quite weary, he sat down, but alas and alack, his fine hat was on the chair and he crushed it completely. "A regular pancake!" said Zephir. Cornelius was aghast, and sadly looked at what was left of his hat. What would he wear on the next formal occasion?

The Old Lady promises Cornelius to sew some plumes on
his old derby, and in order to console him further, she
invites him to go for a ride on the new merry-go-round
which Babar has just had built.

Podular has carved the animals, Justinien has painted them, and the motor was installed by Olur. All three of them are very skillful. They have also made the King's mechanical horse. Olur has just oiled it and Babar is winding it up. He wants to give it a final trial before the big celebration on the anniversary of the founding of Celesteville.

The weather is perfect the day of the celebration. Arthur marches at the head of the parade with Zephir and the band. Cornelius follows, his hat

completely transformed. Then come the soldiers and the trades companies. All those who are not marching are watching this unforgettable spectacle.

On his way home from the celebration Zephir notices a curious stick.

He goes to pick it up. Horrors! It is a snake which rears its head and hisses,

and cruelly bites the Old Lady who tries to hide Zephir in her arms.

Arthur furiously smashes his bugle on the snake's back and kills it.

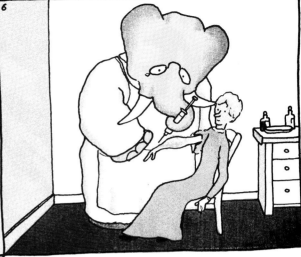

The Old Lady's arm swells rapidly, and she hastens to the hospital.

Dr. Capoulosse takes care of her, and gives her a hypodermic of serum.

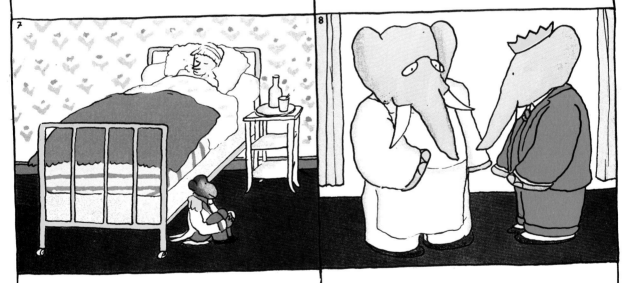

Zephir sadly remains near his mistress. She is very ill.

"I can't tell you until tomorrow whether she will get well," Capoulosse says to Babar.

As Babar leaves the hospital, he hears cries of "Fire! Fire!"
Cornelius' house is on fire. The stairway is already full of
smoke; the firemen succeed in rescuing Cornelius, but he
is half suffocated and a burning beam has injured him.
Capoulosse, summoned in great haste, gives him first-aid
before having him moved to the hospital. A match which
Cornelius thought he had thrown into the ashtray but
which had actually fallen, still lighted, in the trashbasket,
had been enough to start this terrible fire.

That night when Babar goes to bed, he shuts his eyes but
cannot sleep. "What a dreadful day!" he thinks. "It began
so well. Why did it have to end so badly? Before these two
accidents we were all so happy and peaceful at Celesteville!

"We had forgotten that misfortune existed! Oh my dear old Cornelius, and you, dear Old Lady, I would give my crown to see you cured. Capoulosse was to telephone me any news. Oh! How long this night seems, and how worried I am!"

. . . .

Babar finally drops off to sleep, but his sleep is restless and soon *he dreams:* He hears a knocking on his door. Tap! Tap! Tap! Then a voice says to him: "It is I, Misfortune, with some of my companions, come to pay you a visit." Babar looks out of the window, and sees a frightful old woman surrounded by flabby ugly beasts. He opens his mouth to shout: "Ugh! Faugh! Go away quickly!" But he stops to listen to a very faint noise — *Frr! Frr! Frr!* — as of birds flying in a flock, and he sees coming toward him . . .

. . . graceful winged elephants who chase Misfortune away from Celesteville and bring back Happiness. At this point he awakes, and feels ever so much better.

Babar dresses and runs to the hospital. Oh joy! What does he see? His two patients walking in the garden. He can hardly believe his eyes. "We are all well again," says Cornelius, "but all this excitement has made me as hungry as a wolf. Let's get some breakfast, and then later we'll rebuild my house."

A week later, in Babar's drawing room, the Old Lady says to her two friends: "Do you see how in this life one must never be discouraged? The vicious snake didn't kill me, and Cornelius is completely recovered. Let's work hard and cheerfully and we'll continue to be happy."

And since that day, over in the elephant's country, everyone has been happy and contented.

JEAN DE BRUNHOFF
BABAR AND ZEPHIR

Translated from the French by Merle S. Haas

Random House ⌂ New York

The elephants' school at Celesteville is closed
for the whole summer. Zephir, the little monkey,
as well as his bigger schoolmates, goes off for the
holidays. What fun to go and see his family again!
But how sad to leave his friends, King Babar,
Queen Celeste, the Old Lady, his teacher, and his
beloved Arthur!

All four have promised to come to the river
near the bridge to see him off and bid him a last
fond farewell. There they are. Zephir catches
sight of them. He waves his handkerchief and
calls out: "Au revoir!"

Zephir arrives at the station of Monkeyville
and throws himself into his mother's arms.

"Gracious! How you've grown, my darling!"
she says, as she kisses him on both cheeks.

Everybody has piled into the family car. Zephir rides in front next to his father; his mother rides in back with his little sister and his brothers.

"Let's go! Step on the gas!" says Zephir.

They have to use a rope ladder to climb up to the house perched there in the treetops. Zephir scrambles up easily, but laughs as he says to himself: "This wouldn't do at all for my friends the elephants."

The house is small but comfortable. While his mother prepares a good soup of bananas and chocolate, Zephir plays hide and seek with his brothers. His father carries up the baggage, and little sister swings to and fro.

Zephir falls asleep almost as soon as his head
touches the pillow. But in the middle of the night,
the nightingale wakes him with his song: "Trou-
lala, tiou-tiou-tiou! Tidi! Tidi!"

Zephir gets up gaily, and runs to the window.
"Hello, old chap!"

The two cronies now have a little chat.

"Do you know what? There's a big package for you at the station," says the nightingale breathlessly. "On the label is written: 'From Babar'."

"Maybe it's a piano," answers Zephir. "I won first prize in music, you know."

Next morning Zephir hurries to the station. What a wonderful surprise! King Babar has sent him a real rowboat. Zephir, with his father's help, rolls it into the water.

He's going in for a swim, and then later will fish. The elephants have

taught him how. The monkeys admire his courage, for they themselves are afraid of the water.

Princess Isabelle, turning to her father, General Huc, says: "Oh, what a daredevil that fellow Zephir is!"

"What's this I've caught?" Zephir asks himself, greatly surprised. And then the beautiful creature speaks:

"Oh, Mr. Monkey," she says, "don't squeeze me so hard; you're choking me. Listen to me, I pray. I'm a tiny little mermaid, and live in the sea. I have a head and arms, just like you; but see, I have a fish's tail. I'm accustomed to my life in the ocean waves. If you carry me off into the forest, I'll surely die. Leave me here to swim about with my sisters. My name is Eléonore. Maybe, some day, you'll have need of me. If so, throw three pebbles into the water, and repeat my name three times. No matter where I am, I'll hear you and come to you. I will never forget you."

Zephir listens to the mermaid, and then gently frees her from the fish hook. He has just let her go, but is a little sad at having lost her.

On his way home, Zephir sees some monkeys reading the newspapers in the street, and hears the newsboy shouting: "Extra! Extra! Princess Isabelle vanishes!"

"Poor little thing," thinks Zephir. "It can't be true! She was on the beach this morning when I started out to fish."

He listens to the passers-by, and this is what he hears: Isabelle was playing in the palace gardens, when suddenly she was surrounded by a green cloud which wrapped itself around her, hiding her from her friends. Then the cloud rose, leaving behind it a strong odor of rotting apples. The princess hadn't been seen since.

General Huc, full of anxiety and despair, calls out his guardsmen, and gives Colonel Aristobald his orders.

"General," this brave officer replies, "I promise we will do our very best to find your daughter, the princess."

By air, by water, from the treetops and the mountain peaks, even through the underbrush, Aristobald and his soldiers hunt for the princess. In spite of all their efforts, they find no trace of her.

General Huc arrives in his car to get the latest news. When questioned, the colonel lowers his head sadly. The general understands what this means, and goes away with a heavy heart.

Zephir is the only one who doesn't give up hope. Secretly, he puts a gourd and some provisions into his knapsack. He also takes with him his most prized possessions: his violin and his clown costume. Then he starts off toward the sea. Luckily the beach is deserted. He picks up three pebbles, throws them into the water and calls out three times: "Eléonore, my friend, Zephir awaits you here!"

Instantly, just as she had promised, the little mermaid appears.

"Isabelle is lost! Can you help me find her?" asks Zephir.

"That will be difficult," she answers. "But for your sake I'm willing to try. Wait here; I'll go and get my carriage."

A few minutes later Zephir is happily seated in a gigantic sea-going shell. They are off! The racing fish pull them along speedily. Eléonore guides them toward a wild-looking island, and points it out, saying: "That's where my Aunt Crustadele lives. Let's visit her in her grotto; she will give us good advice."

"My children," said Crustadele, after listening to them in silence, "he who smells of rotting apples, he who carried off Isabelle, must be Polomoche."

"Who is Polomoche?" asks Zephir.

"He is a monster who lives on his island with his friends the Gogottes. They live on herbs and fruits, and are not savage. But they are bored.

"From time to time, in order to amuse himself, Polomoche goes off for a trip in a little green cloud. If he meets anyone he likes, he carries him off to his cave. That's what has happened to Isabelle. He is capricious, impatient, and has a bad habit of turning to stone those who anger him.

"Little monkey, if you want to save your princess, there's not a moment to lose. Eléonore will drive you there and wait for you. Take this old sack; it will prove useful.

"And remember, in order to succeed, you'll have to make Polomoche laugh. You'll recognize him by his pointed horns and his yellow skin.

"Leave at once, and good luck to you!"

After a good crossing, Eléonore and Zephir land without being seen by the Gogottes. The country looks bleak. They are now silently taking leave of each other. Zephir holds his friend's little hand in his own.

Zephir puts on Crustadele's sack. It covers him and his few belongings completely, and he immediately resembles the rocks which are scattered all over the island. He walks cautiously to the top of the hill, while working out his plans.

When he gets to the top, he hears a gruff voice. Quickly removing the sack, he peeks through the rocks. There is Isabelle, right in the midst of the monsters!

"Little monkey," growls Polomoche, "I carried you off because I thought you'd be amusing, and here you do nothing but cry! I've had enough of this. I'm going to change you into a rock!"

"Lord Polomoche, and you, Ladies and Gentlemen, permit me to salute you!" says the brave Zephir, politely, as he suddenly emerges from behind the rocks. "I am a clown-musician by profession. Pray allow me to stop here a while, to try to entertain you."

Isabelle, recognizing him, drops her handkerchief and thinks to herself: "Ah! He has come just in the nick of time!"

Pretty soon, thanks to Zephir, everyone is at
ease. A pleasant air of gaiety prevails. He tells
them stories: one about the rat with an elephant's
trunk; one about the blind huntsman; one about
Captain Hoplala and the gun made of macaroni;
and one about Percefeuille and Filigrane. Each
time he finishes a tale, Polomoche and the Gogottes cry: "Tell us another! Tell us one more!"

Tired of talking, Zephir now dons his clown costume. What luck to have brought it with him!

"Presto!"

"There he is!"

"I'm now going to show you a game, 'the chase of the magic hat'."

Having said these words, Bang! Crash! he falls down and turns several somersaults at top speed, and then, when he catches his hat with his tail, Polomoche bursts out laughing heartily.

"That's fine!" thinks the crafty Zephir. "One more little stunt, and the time will be ripe for action. My plan is a good one. By tomorrow we will be far away."

Then, picking up his violin, he plays waltzes and polkas, one after the other. Carried away by the music, they all jump and whirl about giddily.

At last, tired out, they all roll over in a heap and go to sleep, and start to snore peacefully. Zephir takes off his costume and prepares to escape.

"The moment has come!" he whispers to Isabelle, and they dash off to the sea, as fast as their legs can carry them. Eléonore is waiting and waves to them.

They are saved! Land is in sight!

On their way back they stop to thank Crustadele. Some
birds have announced their return, and the news travels fast.

Polomoche and the Gogottes sleep on.

The monkeys come running from all directions. Some
run down to the beach, others watch from the cliff. General
Huc takes out his spy-glass. Zephir's family cries for joy.

Zephir and Isabelle are warmly greeted by the enthusiastic crowd, who shower them with flowers. They've said good-by to the gentle Eléonore, who has gone back home with her fish.

The general congratulates Zephir in front of the soldiers of his guard, and says: "My young friend, I, General Huc, President of the Republic of the Monkeys, am proud of you, and give you my beloved daughter, Isabelle. You may marry her later on, when you become of age."

After this ceremony, when Zephir goes home, his father and his mother, his sister and his brothers, all make a big fuss over him too. They are so happy to see him again that they don't scold him for having gone off without telling them and causing them so much concern. They dance around with him and sing: "Long live the betrothed!"

After starting off with this astonishing adventure, the rest of the holidays pass peacefully and happily. Zephir goes back to Celesteville. As long as he lives with the elephants, Eléonore and her sisters will watch over Isabelle.

JEAN DE BRUNHOFF

BABAR
AND HIS CHILDREN

Translated from the French by Merle S. Haas

Random House 🏠 New York

One morning Babar said to Cornelius: "Old Friend,
you who have been my constant companion through
good times and bad, listen now to my wonderful news.
Celeste, my wife, has just told me that she is expecting
a baby."

Then, pointing to the footstool, he continued: "Here
is a new hat for you and also a message I have just written to my subjects. Take it and read it to all the inhabitants of Celesteville."

After having congratulated and thanked Babar, Cornelius puts
on his full-dress uniform. Standing before the gateway of the
Royal Palace, he tells his drummer to assemble the townspeople.

Slowly he unfurls the King's proclamation, puts on his spectacles, and reads in a loud voice. The elephants, gathered together in large numbers, listen respectfully.

Dear and Loyal Subjects

When you hear a salute fired from a cannon, do not be alarmed. It will not mean that another war has begun, but simply that a little baby has been born to your King and Queen in the Royal Palace.

In this way you will all learn the glorious tidings at the same time.

Long live the future Mother, your Queen Celeste!

Babar

Here, reproduced exactly, is Babar's message, which Cornelius read.

Babar is trying to read, but finds it difficult to concentrate; his thoughts are elsewhere. He tries to write, but again his thoughts wander. He is thinking of his wife and the little baby soon to be born. Will it be handsome and strong? Oh, how hard it is to wait for one's heart's desire!

Celeste urges him to go for a ride on his bicycle, to take his mind off the big event, and Babar finally consents.

After having pedalled several miles, he finds a pleasant spot and decides to rest. Seated on the grass, he admires the surrounding countryside, Celesteville and Fort Saint John. "It is from there that the cannon will be fired," he says to himself.

At this very moment: **Boom!** Babar hears the salute. "There it goes! What a shame that I wasn't at home!" thinks Babar. He immediately mounts his bicycle and rides home as fast as he can pedal.

There, up on the turret, the Artillery Captain of the King's Guard carries out the orders he has just received by telephone. He gives the command. One blank shot is fired, then another and finally a third.

The elephants gather in groups on the promenade and begin to wonder and ask questions. King Babar had only mentioned one shot. Why did the gunners fire off three? Cornelius himself cannot understand it.

Babar reaches home quite breathless from his fast ride. He also had heard three shots. He dashes headlong up the stairs, joyfully rushes into Celeste's bedchamber and embraces his wife tenderly.

She smiles and proudly shows him three little baby elephants. That explains everything. One salute for each child; three babies=three salutes. But what a surprise to find three babies when you only expected one!

The Old Lady has one in her arms, and the nurse holds the other two. Arthur and Zephir are terribly excited. Babar has given them permission to come and see the babies. They walk in quietly. "Oh! How tiny!" says Zephir. "Oh! How cute!" adds Arthur, as he admires the baby lying in the cradle.

Celeste had prepared only one cradle; so the nurse quickly makes another one out of a wash basket, a towel and an umbrella. It is crude, but the babies are warm and sheltered.

Here are the babies, settled now in the garden and asleep in a big perambulator. Babar and Celeste receive the congratulations of their friends. Almost everyone brings a gift.

Poutifour, the farmer, and his wife bring fruits from their own orchard; the hens offer some eggs; the gardener some flowers. The bakers present a huge cake, and Cornelius brings three silver rattles.

Now Babar and Celeste have to find three names for
their children. Of course they had discussed this before-
hand. Pom, Pat or Peter? Julius, John or Jim? Alexander? Emil? Baptiste? Alexander isn't bad, but what if
it's a girl? Juliet, Virginia or . . .

"We'll simply have to come to a decision about their
names," says Celeste to Babar. "I'd like our daughter to
be named Flora."

"I'd like that too," says Babar, "and as for the two
boys, I think we might choose Pom and Alexander."

After having repeated Pom, Flora and Alexander in
one voice, Babar and Celeste declare: "That's perfect.
Let's keep these names."

Every week Dr. Capoulosse puts the babies in his big scale and weighs them. One day he says to Celeste: "Your Majesty, the babies aren't gaining fast enough any more. You must supplement their feeding with six bottles of cow's milk, to which you must add a tablespoonful of honey."

The little ones soon get used to the bottles. Arthur and Zephir like to watch them drink. Pom is the greediest and the fattest. He is the one on Celeste's lap. He always cries when his bottle is empty.

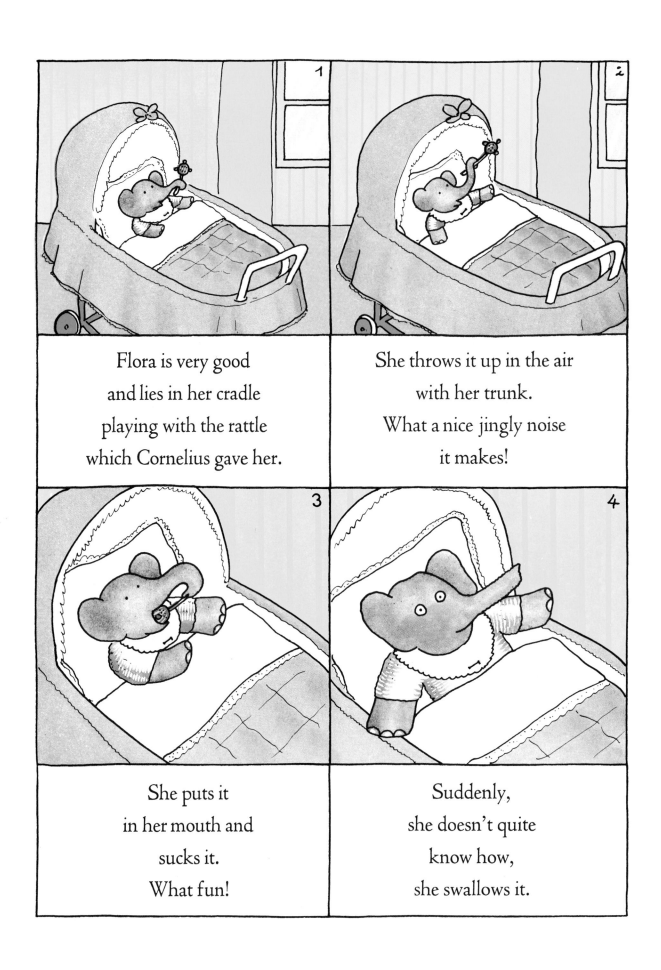

1 Flora is very good and lies in her cradle playing with the rattle which Cornelius gave her.

2 She throws it up in the air with her trunk. What a nice jingly noise it makes!

3 She puts it in her mouth and sucks it. What fun!

4 Suddenly, she doesn't quite know how, she swallows it.

She chokes,
gets purple in the face,
and her trunk trembles.
Celeste rushes to her.

She grabs her, turns her
upside down and shakes
her. But still the rattle
won't fall out.

Fortunately
Zephir manages to
pull it out
with his hand.

Flora is saved, but
she cries most bitterly.
Her mother tries
to comfort her.

Now the children begin to run about and play in their big sunny nursery. Babar often comes in to play with them. Today he sits Pom on the end of his trunk and bounces him up and down. It's like our game "Ride a Cock Horse."

Cornelius hangs the ropes of a swing from the end of each tusk and Arthur gently rocks Alexander back and forth. The boys have learned to walk before their sister. Flora will soon follow their example. She can stand up alone already.

When the children are dressed, the nurse takes them out for a ride in their big carriage. They are still too young to walk very far. One day Nurse says to Arthur: "It is colder than I thought and we are not far from the house. It won't take me long to run back and get some sweaters so my babies won't catch cold. Will you look after them for me until I come back?" Arthur is very glad to be trusted and proudly pushes the carriage.

He pushes it twenty feet forward, then twenty feet back, and takes good care to avoid the stones. All of a sudden he hears the soldiers parading. As he turns around to watch them, he lets go of the pram. The path is slightly downgrade at this point, and the carriage begins to roll off by itself. Pom, Flora and Alexander think this is very funny and laugh, but Arthur is frightened and runs after them. The grade gets steeper and steeper.

The carriage rolls faster and faster. Now the children are scared too. Arthur runs after it as fast as he can. Nurse comes back with the sweaters. Very much worried, she joins the chase. It looks as though the babies are in grave danger. Just a bit farther on there is a bend in the road with a deep ravine on one side. The carriage must be stopped before the bend or it will go straight on down into the ravine, and then . . . The accident! Martha, the turtle, out for a stroll, has seen it all coming and understands the situation thoroughly.

She hurries along on her short legs. Just as the carriage is about to topple over the precipice, she succeeds in throwing herself under the wheels! Suddenly checked while going full tilt, the carriage stops and almost turns over. Pom and Flora are jolted back against the hood, which saves them, but poor Alexander is thrown out head first. Nurse screams and the rabbit runs away.

Mr. and Mrs. Squirrel
have heard the
nurse's scream.
Then, a minute later,
they hear the
rustle of leaves
and the noise of
breaking branches to
the left above them.
They both look up
and see the head of
a baby elephant.
He is yelling for his mother in a frightened lisp.
"Mama! Alessander's falling! Mama! Help Alessander!"

"Steady, little elephant! Don't let go! We're coming!" cry the squirrels. "Just balance yourself and try to get your foot up on that big branch. We're right here. Don't be afraid. We'll help you!"

Their scheme succeeds. Mr. Squirrel gives further orders. "Hold fast to my tail and wiggle your big ears to keep your balance! Watch your step! Follow me! You can rest when you've reached our shelter!" A few minutes later, safe and sound in the squirrels' hole,

Alexander breathes a sigh of relief. How lucky he was to have fallen in the trees, and to have found these obliging friends! He might have been badly hurt! Now he'd like to go and tell his Mama not to worry. But how can he get down that tree trunk? It is absolutely smooth and very high! Just then a big giraffe strolls by and sees his plight. He says: "Look here, little elephant, I'll put my head right close to the branch.

Then you can sit down between my ears and hold on to my horns. I know your parents and I'll take you back to them."

Alexander, quite delighted, says good-by to the squirrels and thanks them. He settles himself on the giraffe's head, and off they go. Although the giraffe walks slowly, Alexander decides that he prefers his perambulator.

Informed by the nurse, Babar and Celeste are already on their way to the scene of the accident. What joy to be reunited! Arthur is ever so pleased.

A few months later, Babar decides it would be fun to go on a picnic. The weather is fine, and the family is in high spirits. Cornelius feels the heat, but joins them enthusiastically. Later, tired and hungry, they all sit down to a delicious lunch.

After the meal Celeste tidies things up. Babar goes off to fish in a nearby stream. Cornelius lies down in the shade to have a nap. Alexander mischievously wriggles under Cornelius' derby hat and walks about with short steps. "That's a funny-looking tortoise!" says Pom.

While playing, they come to the edge of the river. Alexander has another bright idea. He puts the hat in the water. "Nice boat!" says he,
as he steps in to try it. "It floats! Isn't that marvelous?"

Just then the current catches the hat, and it drifts away from the bank. Alexander is enchanted with his boat ride, but Pom and Flora are a bit worried.

How can they get the hat back to shore? Flora begins to cry. She runs off to call her Mama, who was just beginning to wonder where the children could be. Pom runs along the bank calling: "Alexander, come back! Please, nice little ducks, oh, please bring my brother back!"

But the ducks fly away. Suddenly, Pom gives a lusty yell: "A crocodile! A crocodile!"

Alexander looks around. "Oh! Papa!" he whimpers.

Babar was peacefully fishing and thought the children were playing. As he hears this desperate cry for help, he understands that something serious must have happened. He stands up and trumpets angrily as he sees the horrible crocodile.

Three seconds in which to act–and no gun! The situation seems hopeless! Babar, without hesitating a moment, grabs the anchor and hurls it violently into the monster's jaws. Caught like a fish, the crocodile in a wild fit of rage flips his tail right out of the water. Tossed about by the swirling eddy, the hat capsizes and Alexander is thrown into the river.

Babar dives in after him, and searches about with his trunk. Ah! He feels something! Hurrah! It's Alexander's ear! He makes quick work of bringing him up out of the water and reviving him. As for the crocodile, he thrashes madly about, but cannot rid himself of either the anchor or the boat.

The birds gather around Babar and Alexander who are of course dripping wet.

"Would you be kind enough," asks Babar, "to go and reassure Queen Celeste? Ask her to hurry back to the house to lay out some dry clothes and prepare hot drinks for us. And you, dear little ducklings," he adds, "would you be kind enough to dive down and bring back my crown and Cornelius' hat? They are down at the bottom of the river."

Alexander kisses his Mama happily. She bathes him, gives him a good rubdown and puts him to bed under heavy blankets.

Arthur, Zephir, Pom and Flora are still very excited. The big flamingo brings back the crown and the hat. "Oh, thank you very much," says Babar. "The hat is slightly damp and out of shape. Cornelius, however, will be happy to have it back because it is an old keepsake."

Now everyone is asleep. Babar and Celeste will soon go to bed too. They are gradually calming down after all these exciting events.

"Truly it is not easy to bring up a family," sighs Babar. "But how nice the babies are! I wouldn't know how to get along without them any more."

JEAN DE BRUNHOFF

BABAR
AND
FATHER CHRISTMAS

Translated from the French by Merle S. Haas
Random House 🏠 New York

One day Zephir calls to his friends Arthur, Pom, Flora and Alexander:

"Listen, listen to this wonderful tale which I've just heard! It seems that in Man's country, every year, on the night before Christmas, a very kind old gentleman with a large white beard, wearing a red suit with a pointed hood, flies over the countryside. He carries with him great quantities of toys and gives them to the little children. They call him Father Christmas. It is difficult to catch a glimpse of him for he comes down the chimney while one sleeps. Next morning the children know he has been there because they find toys in their shoes. Why shouldn't we write to him and ask him to come here too and see us in the Elephants' country?"

"Three cheers! What a fine idea!" says Alexander. "But what shall we say in the letter?" asks Arthur. "We must write and tell Father Christmas what we would like him to bring us," suggests Pom. "Let's consider very carefully before we write," adds Flora.

They remain quiet a moment and think it over.

Zephir decides a bicycle would be just what he wants, Flora would love to have a doll. Alexander wants a butterfly net, Pom a big bag of candies and a little Teddy Bear. As for Arthur, his dream is to have a train.

Then, each having decided what to wish for, Zephir is chosen to write the letter, for he has the best handwriting. He applies himself to his task. Arthur remembers that a stamp must be put on the envelope. Then they each sign their names and go off together in great glee to mail the letter.

Every morning the five friends eagerly await the postman. They rush out to meet him as soon as they see him coming. But alas, although the postman searches carefully, there is no answer from Father Christmas.

One day Babar happens to see them and says to himself: "Whatever can be the matter with those children? They look so dreadfully sad."

So he calls to them and says: "Come on, tell me what's the matter."

Zephir tells him the story of his letter.

"And you haven't had an answer? Is that it?" asks Babar. "You must have forgotten to put a stamp on it."

"Oh no we didn't, Arthur remembered to."

"Well, then Father Christmas hasn't had time to answer it yet. Cheer up and run along now and play. Possibly you've given me a very excellent idea."

Babar paces thoughtfully up and down, lost in thought. "I wonder why I never thought myself of asking Father Christmas to come to the Elephants' country."

"The best thing to do would be to start out at once to find him. If I ask him personally he will surely not refuse to come."

His mind made up, Babar hurries to inform Celeste of his intentions. She helps him to pack and get ready. She would like very much to go along, but Babar explains to her that she'll be needed at home to rule the country during his absence, and also remarks that queer characters like Father Christmas are often shy, and rarely allow themselves to be approached by more than one person at a time.

Babar arrives in Europe after a very good journey. He has just stepped from the train. In order not to be recognized he has left his crown at home.

He drives to a little old hotel which is clean and quiet, and is given a room which pleases him. Next he undresses and washes up a bit. One always feels so refreshed after a good cleaning up. "What can be making that funny little noise?" wonders Babar as he dries himself off. Without moving he looks around, and all of a sudden he sees three young mice.

The least timid of them says: "Good-day, my stout Sir, are we to have the pleasure of your company for long?"

"Oh no, I'm just passing through. I'm looking for Father Christmas," answers Babar.

"You're looking for Father Christmas.—Why, goodness, he's here in this very house, we know him well. We'll show you his room," chorused the three little mice.

"How wonderful! What really extraordinary luck! Just give me time to put on my dressing gown, and I'll be with you," cries the excited Babar.

"But where on earth are these little mice leading me?" wonders Babar as he stops a moment on the stairs to catch his breath. "Father Christmas must live way up on the top floor. No doubt he likes to have a good view and plenty of open space around him."

While Babar is making these observations, the three little mice reach the attic. Whatever are they doing over there in that corner? They seem all excited!

"Where are you?" calls Babar.

"Up here in the attic," answer the little mice. "Come quickly! We have taken Father Christmas down from the top of the tree."

When Babar joins them, the delighted little mice say:

"There is Father Christmas! He lives here peacefully the whole year round, excepting on Christmas Day when they come and fetch him to hang on top of a new Christmas tree. After the holiday he resumes his place in this corner and we can come and play with him again."

"But this isn't the one I'm looking for; I want to find the real live Father Christmas, not a doll!" says Babar sadly.

Next morning Babar hears a tapping at his window, and sees some sparrows outside on the sill. They speak to him and say:

"We understand that you are searching for the real live Father Christmas. We know him well and are going to take you to him." And off they fly joyously.

Pointing out the way to Babar, they lead him across the big bridge over the river. "We're almost there," they call. "We usually find him around here, he sleeps under the bridges."

"Well, well, that is strange," thinks Babar.

"There he is! There he is!" cry all the little sparrows together. "He's over there next to that fisherman casting his line."

Babar, still a bit astonished at this old fellow's odd appearance, greets him and says: "Excuse me, Sir. But are you really the true Father Christmas, the one who brings toys to all the children?"

"Alas no," answers the old man. "My name is Lazzaro Campeotti. I am an artist's model and my friends the artists have nick-named me Father Christmas. Now every-body calls me by that name."

Very much disappointed, Babar strolls thoughtfully along the river banks.

Stopping at one of the book stalls, Babar finds a book with pictures of Father Christmas. He quickly buys it and takes it back to his room to examine it  more carefully. Unfortunately the text is written in a language which he does not understand. He goes down to explain his difficulty to the hotel manager, who helpfully gives him the address of a professor at the school where his son is studying.

"Mr. Gillianez will surely be able to translate your book," says he.

Without losing a moment, Babar is at the door of Professor Gillianez' house ringing the bell. He finds him at

home but after a glance at the book the Professor says that to his great regret he is unable to read it either. He gives Babar the address of the famous Professor William Jones.

An hour later Babar is in this man's study. The Professor carefully examines the book, and shakes his head gloomily. Finally he turns to Babar who has been waiting patiently, and says: "Your book is very difficult to read. It is written in old style Gothic letters. There are facts in it about the life of Father Christmas, and they say he lives in Bohemia, not far from the little town of PRJMNESWE. But I do not find any more definite information on this point."

Babar goes off and sits on a bench in the public park to think the matter over. The birds recognize him and come over to inquire whether he has found Father Christmas.

"No, not yet," answers Babar. "I only know that he lives far away from here near the town of PRJMNESWE. Truly this is a difficult search."

Just then a little dog who is passing by says to Babar: "Pardon me, Sir. I'm very good at finding things which are lost, because I have a highly developed sense of smell.

"If only I could have a sniff of that doll, which Father Christmas gave to little Virginia over there, I'm sure I'd be able to help you find him. I would be very glad to go with you because I am a little homeless dog."

Upon hearing these words Babar looks at the dog and says: "Agreed, I'll take you along with me."

Then off he goes to buy a beautiful new doll for Virginia which she gladly accepts in exchange for her other one. Babar lets the dog sniff the old doll, and feeds him a piece of candy.

Before starting out Babar goes back to see the learned Professor William Jones who returns his book and gives him a few additional directions. Father Christmas apparently lives in a forest on a mountain about twelve miles from PRJMNESWE.

Babar arrives at the little town after a difficult journey.

It is very cold and a great deal of snow has
fallen. Babar therefore equips himself accord-
ingly. He buys some skis, hires a sleigh and
has himself driven to the foot of the mountain.

Pretty soon he has to get out and, accompanied only by his faithful Duck (this is the
name he has given his dog), he starts to climb
in the direction of the mysterious forest, skis
on his feet, and a heavily laden pack on his
back. Duck is very much excited. He sniffs
here and there and yaps softly. Now he stands
still, his tail lifted, his nose twitching hard.
He must have caught the scent of Father
Christmas.

Suddenly
Duck is
off on the run.
"I've got it!
I've got it!
We're on
the right track."
His loud
barking echoes
through the woods.
But what is that
stirring in
this wild forest?

It is a band of little mountain dwarfs who have hidden themselves behind the tree trunks. Duck would like to see them nearer by, but they rush at him, pelting him fast and furiously with hard-packed snowballs which land on his head, in his eyes and on his sides.

Half choked,
half blinded,
his tail
between his legs,
Duck decides
to retreat.
He quickly runs to
rejoin his master,
and arrives
breathless,
feeling very
foolish.

When Babar sees him he stops short and asks: "What's happened?" Duck then tells him of his adventure with the little bearded dwarfs.

"Good, we must be getting nearer," replies Babar. "I am very eager to meet those dwarfs, lead me to them."

A few minutes later it is Babar's turn to meet the dwarfs. They try to frighten him too, and rush bravely toward him, and pelt him, but Babar calmly takes a deep breath and blows it out hard in their direction. They all tumble down one on top of the other, and as soon as they can scramble back to their feet, off they run and noiselessly disappear.

Babar roars with laughter, and continues on his way, following Duck who has now found the scent again.

The little dwarfs have run to find Father Christmas and they tell him, all jabbering at once, that an enormous animal with a long nose blew on them so hard that he knocked them down and chased them away. Father Christmas listens attentively. The little dwarfs add that when they fled, this big monster was quite near, and that, guided by an ugly little cur, he was heading straight for the secret cave of Father Christmas.

They were right. Babar is nearing the cave, but a storm of extraordinary violence suddenly bursts upon him. The wind blows so hard that the snowflakes prick his eyes and skin. It is impossible to see. Babar struggles desperately; then, realizing the danger of obstinately forging ahead blindly, he decides to dig himself a hole for shelter.

Then he rigs up a roof with his skis and ski-poles and some snow blocks. The two companions are fairly well protected now.

"Whew! It is cold and my trunk is beginning to freeze," thinks Babar. Duck is also cold and tired.

All of a sudden, Babar feels the earth giving away under him, and he and Duck drop out of sight. Where have they fallen?

Without realizing it they have dropped right down through a chimney vent into the cave of Father Christmas. "Father Christmas!" cries the amazed Babar. "Duck, we've arrived at our destination."

Whereupon he faints, worn out with fatigue, the cold and the excitement. "Quick, little mountain dwarfs, forget your quarrel, we must undress him and get him warm," says Father Christmas.

They all set to immediately. They undress him, and give him a good alcohol rub, working over him energetically with big brushes. The dwarf chemist gives him some brandy. Then finally, Babar drinks a fine bowl of hot soup with Father Christmas and thanks him from the bottom of his heart.

While Father Christmas shows him around, Babar explains that he has made this long journey to ask him to visit the Elephants' country.

N.B.—This tour includes the big room in which Father Christmas usually lives; the room into which Babar fell through the hole, which one can see in the upper right-hand corner; and the toy rooms, the doll room, the tin soldier room, the armory with toy guns, the room full of

Won't he distribute toys to the elephant children, just as he does to the children of men? Father Christmas is much touched by this request,

trains, the room with building blocks, the room where the stuffed animals are kept, the one with tennis racquets and balls, etc. (all these things neatly packed in boxes and in bags). And then they visited the dwarfs' dormitories, the elevators worked by pulleys and the machine shop.

but he tells Babar that he will not be able to visit the Elephants' country Christmas night because he is very tired.

He adds: "I had great difficulty last year in completing the usual delivery and distribution of toys to the children all over the world."

"Oh, Father Christmas, I understand perfectly," says Babar, "but if this is the case you must take care of yourself.

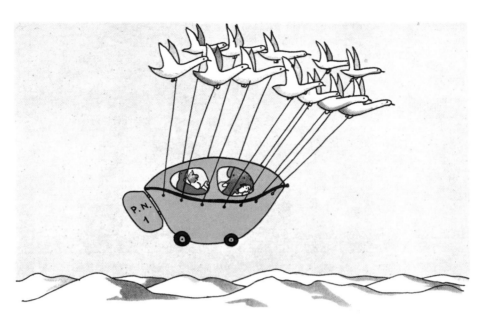

"Why not live on the earth's surface for a while and leave your underground home? Come back with me now to our country and bask in the sun. You will be rested and cured for Christmas."

Charmed by this suggestion, Father Christmas instructs the little dwarfs to keep an eye on everything for him. Then off he goes in his flying machine, accompanied by Babar and Duck.

Here they are in the Elephants' country. Father Christmas admires the countryside and is quickly surrounded by the elephants who rush over to bid him welcome. Pom, Flora and Alexander hurry over too. In order to get the best view, Arthur has climbed to the roof of a house and Zephir is up in a tree.

When the excitement quiets down Queen Celeste introduces her three children and Arthur and Zephir to Father Christmas.

"Oh, you are the ones who wrote me," he says. "I am delighted to meet you and I promise you a Merry Christmas."

Father Christmas
often goes
out riding
on zebra back.
Babar rides
along on
his bicycle.

And Father Christmas takes a sun-bath for two full hours every day, following Dr. Capoulosse's instructions. Sometimes Pom, Flora and Alexander come to watch him as he lies in his hammock, but they are careful to make no noise, so as not to disturb him.

One day
Father Christmas
says to Babar:
"My dear friend,
thank you very
much for all that you
have done for me.

Christmas is nearly here and I must leave to distribute the awaited gifts to the children of men. But I'm not forgetting the promise I made to the little elephants. Can you guess what I have in this bag? A real Santa Claus suit made to your measure! It is a magic suit which will enable you to fly through the air, and your bag will always be full of toys. You can take my place here Christmas Eve. I promise you I'll return when my work is done and I'll bring the children a fine Christmas tree."

On the night before Christmas Babar follows out these instructions. As soon as he puts on the suit and beard, he notices that he instantly becomes lighter and is at the same time able to fly with ease.

"This is really extraordinary! And what a good way to distribute all the gifts to the children!" thinks Babar.

He hurries in order to get through with his task before dawn. What joy there will be in every house on Christmas morning when the little elephants awake!

In the royal palace Queen Celeste peeks through the door of the children's room. Pom is emptying his stocking, Flora is rocking her doll, and Alexander is jumping up and down on his bed, exclaiming: "What a wonderful Christmas! What a wonderful Christmas!"

As he had promised, Father Christmas has come back
bringing them a beautiful Christmas tree. And thanks to
him the family celebration is a great success.

Arthur, Zephir, Pom, Flora and Alexander have never seen anything as beautiful as this fir tree all shining with lights.

Next day, Father Christmas flies away again in his airplane to rejoin his little subjects, the dwarfs, in his underground palace.

On the banks of the big lake, Babar, Celeste, Arthur, Zephir, and the three children sadly wave their handker-chiefs.

Fortunately, Father Christmas has promised to come back to the Elephants' country every year.

About JEAN DE BRUNHOFF

Jean de Brunhoff was born in 1899 in France and was already an accomplished painter and the father of two young sons when he created his first book about Babar in 1931. It was actually his wife, Cécile, who one day in 1930 invented the bare bones of *The Story of Babar* to amuse her boys, Mathieu and Laurent. Their enthusiastic retelling of the story of the little elephant who lost his mother and ran away to Paris inspired Jean de Brunhoff to turn it into a big illustrated storybook. From 1931 to 1937, he created six Babar storybooks, all of which are reproduced— word for word, picture for picture—in this gift edition. In addition to the six stories, he also created *The ABC's of Babar* in 1934.

Jean de Brunhoff died of tuberculosis in 1937 at the early age of thirty-seven. At the time of his death he had completed the stories and the line drawings for *Babar and His Children* and *Babar and Father Christmas*. His brother Michel, who was the editor-in-chief of the French *Vogue,* directed the coloring of these last two books. Laurent de Brunhoff, who was only twelve years old when his father died but knew already that he would become a painter, was allowed to color in a few of these pages. Shortly after World War II, Laurent began creating his own books about the world's most beloved elephant.

Often referred to as the father of the contemporary picture book, Jean de Brunhoff—with his sure combination of graphic art and storytelling—has inspired generations of children's book author-artists the world over. This volume is a celebration of his great contribution to children's literature, with thanks to his son Laurent for carrying on the tradition.